·MEANWHILE·
Back at the Ranch

·MEANWHILE·
Back at the Ranch

Trinka Hakes Noble / *pictures by* Tony Ross

DIAL BOOKS FOR YOUNG READERS *New York*

92030

Published by Dial Books for Young Readers
2 Park Avenue
New York, New York 10016

Published simultaneously in Canada by Fitzhenry & Whiteside Limited, Toronto
Text copyright © 1987 by Trinka Hakes Noble
Pictures copyright © 1987 by Tony Ross
All rights reserved
Printed in Hong Kong by South China Printing Co.
Typography by Sara Reynolds
First Edition
W
2 4 6 8 10 9 7 5 3 1

Library of Congress Cataloging-in-Publication Data
Noble, Trinka Hakes. Meanwhile back at the ranch.
Summary: Looking for some diversion, a bored rancher drives
to the town of Sleepy Gulch little knowing that some amazing things
are happening to his wife and ranch during his absence.
[1. Ranch life—Fiction. 2. Humorous stories.]
I. Ross, Tony, ill. II. Title.
PZ7.N6715Me 1987 [E] 86-11651
ISBN: 0-8037-0353-8
ISBN: 0-8037-0354-6 (lib. bdg.)

For Judy, with love   T. H. N.

To Klaus   T. R.

Rancher Hicks lived out west. As far as the eye could see there was nothing...not even a roaming buffalo. So nothing much ever happened.

"I think I'll drive into town and see what's happening," said
 Rancher Hicks.
"Want to ride along, Elna?" he asked his wife.
"No. I've got to dig potatoes," said Elna.

So Rancher Hicks climbed into his truck and drove eighty-four miles to the town of Sleepy Gulch.
He stopped at the post office to look at the new wanted posters, but they were the same ones that were there twelve years ago.

Meanwhile...back at the ranch...
The cat had just had kittens in Elna's sewing basket when the phone rang.

"Hello?"

"Mrs. Elna Hicks?"

"Yes."

"Mrs. Hicks, you have just won a brand-new wall-to-wall frost-free super-cool refrigerator with a built-in automatic food maker!"

"Why I never!" exclaimed Elna.

"The delivery men are on their way."

Meanwhile…*yawn*…back in Sleepy Gulch…
Rancher Hicks strolled on over to the barber shop for a whisker
trim and to hear the latest gossip.
"So what's new, Bob?" asked Rancher Hicks.
"Well…back in the spring of '49 we had a rainstorm you wouldn't
believe. Why, it rained for pretty near a whole five minutes. Folks
thought it'd never stop. Nothin' much been happening since."

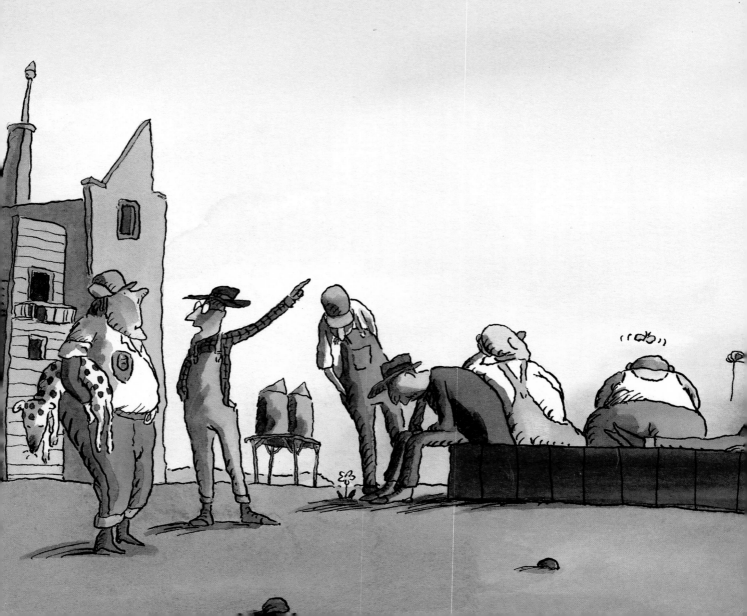

Meanwhile...back at the ranch...
The dog had just had puppies when the postman came up
the drive with a special delivery.
Elna opened it.

It was her Great Aunt Edith's will. It said:

My dear Elna,
I am leaving you my entire estate which is worth a bundle.
                         Your loving Great Aunt Edith
P.S. Enclosed is a winning lottery ticket. I didn't have time
to cash it in.

So Elna cashed in the lottery ticket and put new siding on the house. Then she added a new wing for the wall-to-wall refrigerator and a new den for all the puppies and kittens.

Meanwhile...*snore*...back in Sleepy Gulch...
Rancher Hicks mosied on over to Millie's Mildew Luncheonette.
"What's on the menu for today, Millie?"
"Well, we got potatoes mashed and potatoes fried, potatoes boiled
and potatoes baked, potatoes roasted and potatoes stewed,
potatoes scalloped and potatoes steamed, and one egg."
"Sounds great," said Rancher Hicks. "I'll have one of each and
a side order of fries."

Meanwhile...back at the ranch...
After all the pigs had had piglets, Elna finally started to dig
potatoes. She struck oil!

The oilmen came and gave her lots of money. They started eight
new oil wells and an oil refinery that day!
Elna took the money and had a very stylish sty built for all the
pigs and piglets.

Meanwhile…*sigh*…back in Sleepy Gulch…
Rancher Hicks headed on over to the general store to check out
the checker game.

"Howdy, boys. What's new?"

"Well, Bernie here just got a king and it only took him two weeks!"
said Kurt.

"And I just jumped two of Kurt's men in a little over two hours!"
said Bernie.

"Wow. What a game!" said Rancher Hicks. "I can't wait to
tell Elna."

Meanwhile...back at the ranch...
All the cows had calves when a silver limo swung into the
driveway. Out jumped a Hollywood movie producer and
his hairdresser.

"Elna Hicks, I'm going to make you a movie star!"

So Elna went on a diet and lost twenty pounds. The hairdresser dyed her hair blond and painted her lips red.

The movie producer gave her a script, a bikini, and a large stack of dollar bills!

So Elna had a glamorous cow palace built for all the cows and calves, and she studied her script.

Meanwhile...*ho hum*...back in Sleepy Gulch...
Rancher Hicks started to cross Main Street when he saw it!
"Amazing," he gasped.
Folks ran to see it.
"Incredible," they said.

A crowd gathered.

"This is big news, really big," said the newspaper editor.

"We'd better wake up the mayor," said the sheriff.

The mayor came. "Why I've never seen anything like it!" said the mayor. So he declared it a town holiday.

The whole town watched it for hours and hours until finally...

a turtle crossed Main Street!!

Meanwhile…back at the ranch…
All the horses had colts when the President's helicopter landed in Elna's yard. "Elna Hicks," he said, "you've got the finest horses west of Washington. I'm making you a diplomat. Please deliver two of your finest horses to the Queen of England!"
The President paid Elna for the horses and gave her a diplomat's diploma and an autographed picture of himself. "Don't forget to vote for me!"
Elna took the money and had a very stately stable built for all the horses and colts.

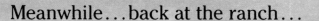

Meanwhile... *zzzzzzz*...back in Sleepy Gulch...
The sun began to sink slowly in the west. Rancher Hicks felt bad
that Elna had missed all the excitement so he stopped and
bought her a box of Cracker Jacks.
"This will make her day," he said.
Then he climbed into his truck and drove eighty-four miles back
to the ranch.

Elna met Rancher Hicks down by the mailbox.

He gave her the box of Cracker Jacks and told her about all the excitement.

"Shoot! I miss everything," said Elna.

Then Rancher Hicks turned around.

"What the hay...?!?!??!"